Other books published by this author

The Adventures of Chocolate Sunshine

CHERREL TURNER-CALLWOOD

THE JOURNEY

OF

AN INVISIBLE BROWN GIRL

Skinulicious Services Books

THE JOURNEY OF AN INVISIBLE BROWN GIRL

CHERREL TURNER-CALLWOOD

ISBN:978-0-9977601-1-8

SKINULICIOUS SERVICES PUBLISHING

Clearwater, Florida 33760

United States of America

Today is as good as any day to share this journey. There is so much, to this journey called life, that others do not want to see. This is for all the invisibles walking around! This is also for all of those who wanted me to be quiet; to keep it a secret! Sometimes, the truth must be told! Ctc

Any similarities to events, characters and places is strictly coincidental!!

CONTENT

Learning the truth, to many, now means justifying behavior when the lie was believed!

CHERREL TURNER-CALLWOOD

The Tears of a Child

To be born into this world

so innocent and so pure

a bouncing baby boy or a girl

to be delivered to parents so unsure

the tears of a child

Wanting the attention and the love

the kisses the hugs

that God had promised us from above

only to be pushed and shoved

the tears of a child

To be beat and punched, kicked and slapped

accepting this *abuse as a way of life*

learning to hate and to fight back

being touched and fondled by a father who didn't

care for my life

the tears of a child

Searching for love in all places

Clubs, jobs, family, spouse

looking for someone to fill empty spaces

feeling threatened and afraid like a mouse

the tears of a child

growing up to be an adult

with so much love to give

trying to hold on to faith, dreams with results

just so I can go on with life, so I can live

the tears of a child

God is good, God is so real

God gives me the love I need

God is helping me to heal

when I'm hungry for love, I won't be afraid to feel

the tears of a child

This invisible brown girl was born at the end of the 1950s. I, Destiny, didn't learn till later that I was not wanted. This invisible brown girl was informed that she was the result of a sexual union between two people. Wow! So, did Destiny really have a say so in this matter? Was the marriage between her parents her fault? Destiny always wondered, being invisible, how she made them have sex.

I, Destiny, do not remember much about the first few years of my life. I do remember my father used to beat my mother alot. I also remember when my mother left my father for good.

My mother, along with my brother Daniel and I, relocated to the projects. I learned very early that I was invisible. My mother worked all the time and was very bitter of the way her life was going with two children. She constantly reminded me that she had to get married because she was pregnant with me or that abortions weren't easy to get back in them days. She really hated me.

I never learned how to be a child. When my mother had to work, at night, she would lock Daniel and I in our room. We probably were about 9 or 10 years old. We were children and did get into things when she went to work. My brother and I would take the mattress off our bed and slide down the steps. There would be candy in her room and we would break the lock on her door to get it. There were times that the house would get robbed while my brother and I were locked in our room. We even tried to run away, but, I got scared to climb out of a second-floor window. How many people knew that we were locked in our room and being abused but looked the other way?

I remember wishing I was invisible when my mother started physically and verbally abusing me. She hated me and let me know every chance she could. She would beat me with sticks, belts or whatever she could find. I remember one time being beat, on the hand, with a stick. I went to school with my hand swollen. Destiny played the violin at the time. I recall my violin teacher squeezing my hand, so I could hold the bow correctly. However, she never said anything about my swollen hands. My hands must have been invisible.

Destiny remembers another time when she was in her mother's room and accidently knocked her make-up mirror on the floor. It broke. My mother beat me with a stick, busting my foot. The scar is still there today. I also have scars on my leg from being stabbed with a two-prong fork. It is just obvious that some people are not meant to be parents. The news shows this fact like every day. These are just some of the abuses I experienced during my childhood. I know there were things that I did as a child that was mischievous, but, it did not mean for me to be hated.

My mother is always quick to say that we never got along, but, where does this come from? A parent and child are supposed to be on two different levels. The problem comes into play when the parent expects a minor child to act like an adult. Your job, as a parent, is to mold your child to become a future adult. Showing hate, being abusive, and instilling fear are not grounds for molding a child. It is even worse when a parent includes others in the abuse of a child. I would later find out that other women would tell my mother that I was messing with their men. Destiny was no older than ten years old. I did not realize then that this was a sign of adults being cowards, insecure, and trifling. I also would learn that everyone has a right to their own story. The truth is only known by God.

Even though the invisible brown girl endured a lot of abuse, she is very smart as well as talented. I learned how to sing, play the violin, the piano, and the organ. I was also a great swimmer. My brother and I were never allowed to call our mother "mom". I do not recall ever being told she loved us. Destiny felt truly invisible.

Throwing out trash

After being abused, up until this point, Destiny was then sent to stay with her father. She thought life would finally be wonderful. Destiny eventually would learn that this was not true.

My father lived with his girlfriend. Carla had three children; two who were by my father. The youngest girl was my baby sister and I immediately fell for her. I enjoyed feeding her as well as playing with her. I really was enjoying things at this house. I was convinced that I was wanted and love. I later learned that this was all a disguise.

Destiny had her 12th birthday with them. What is so interesting is that there are moments, in my life, that I do not remember. Like, I don't remember getting anything for my birthdays nor for Christmas. I also do not recall where was my brother Daniel. Somewhere, around this time, I did realize that my existence on Earth was just to be a punishment.

During this time, I learned that no one liked me. My father and his girlfriend would drink almost every weekend with family as well as with their friends. They would drink until they would be drunk. Destiny recalled one of these drinking encounters would alter the rest of her life.

While getting adjusted to my new living environment, I always got stuck babysitting everyone's children. I recalled that Carla's birthday was in the month of January. So, she along with some other adults, would get drunk during this time. I do not know what happened, but, Carla's daughter and I got into trouble over something. She and I never got along. She would always pick on me knowing that I would get in trouble if I did anything to her. She never got in trouble for being mean towards me. This night, we were about to be punished. She got a beating and was sent to bed. I thought I was next for a beating.

My stepmother was out somewhere, and the other children were sleep. My father called me into his bedroom. I thought I was about to get a beating, but it turned out to be something worse. My father had me take off my pajamas and told me to get on the bed. He took his penis out of his pants and proceeded to penetrate Destiny. She was a virgin at the time. It was painful, but I was too afraid to move or scream. He then attempted to penetrate me again after using some shampoo to lubricate his penis but had no luck. He told me that I was just like my mother was when he first messed with her. I had completely zoned out. After he got tired of trying to penetrate me, he sent me to bed. I think I went to bed and just blacked out.

The next day, when everyone else was out of the house, my father called me upstairs while he was shaving. I though he was going to repeat what he did the night before. He instead told me he was sorry and that he was drunk. Even at the age of 12, I knew a person knows what they do and say when they are drunk.

I am not exactly sure of what took place, but, I later would run away to one of my aunt's house. I told my Aunt Jane what her brother had done to me. She had me to call my mother. When I called my mother, I told her everything thing that happened to me. She told me that sounds like something he would do but she couldn't take me back. My mother does not recall this incident. She becomes very hostile when I mentioned this to her. She said that no one never called her. She later would add that I probably did not tell her because she would have told the authorities and that I thought that they would send me back to her since we did not get along. My mother told me that I could have went to a foster home. What kind of crap is this to tell your child? So basically, Destiny was the blamed for what

happened to her. Putting me in foster care would have kept me invisible. Her mother asked her, "What kind of mother would that had made her?" Duh, the kind of mother who never wanted her child. The one she wanted invisible; the one she did not love!

"PAT"

Pain and

Agony

Tears and defeat

Touching me all over

As though I was a piece of meat

Abandonment and abuse

Drunk and unstable

Being forced on a table

How could you be so wrapped up in yourself

Ignoring the cries, warnings, and clues

Why didn't you act like a mother without a doubt

Protecting your child who was a gift to you

Unloved

After that ordeal, Destiny was sent back to her father's house. I was put on punishment and life got worse. I do not recall too much of a childhood. My life, as a child, was totally invisible. I do remember doing some childhood things like jumping rope, playing jaxs and other games outdoors. I was the queen of double dutch; or so I thought so. I learned playing cards when my brother and I lived with our mother. We played pinochle. It was not fun. My mother would have a stick, and when we made an error, she would whack us with the stick. We eventually became good at playing these games.

I always took care of everyone's children while they enjoyed their lives. These children were bad and never listen to me. I couldn't do anything to them without the fear that I would get in trouble. After all, I was just a small, frail child myself. Destiny was an invisible brown girl that no one knew existed.

I always had chores to do, errands or whatever was needed to make life easier for everyone. A substitute for their adult needs. I did enjoy music and dancing. These were the means of escape for me. When I needed to zone out, I would hum some tunes. I still do this today. The funny thing is that these tunes, I never heard them. I knew all the new dances, from watching Soul Train, and enjoyed showing everyone my skills. I also enjoyed reading. It was my escape and my adventures from the real world. Outside of relatives, I only had two friends that I would see whenever I could go outside. However, these fun times were very few in between. No one liked me or loved me. If they did, I was never told. By the time I was fourteen, I had been on punishment and beat for everything. However, what took place next should not have been a surprised to me.

"O' Christmas Tree"

O' Christmas tree

O' Christmas tree

How lovely are thy branches

O' Christmas tree

O' Christmas tree

He touched me every chances

You stood so green with flashing lights

While he screwed me in the night

O' Christmas tree

O' Christmas tree

How lovely are thy branches

Unlike many journeys, mines do not use dates. Why? Well, some of life experiences do not get documented when they happen. However, it is still my journey.

I do not know the exact date, but I do know that the next event took place around the Christmas holiday. I remember that my stepmother was upstairs drunk and everyone else was sleep except for me. I probably was doing dishes or some chore. I recall my father putting me on top of the table, in the dining room. With my underwear down, he performed oral sex on me. He then took me in the living room, and sitting next to the Christmas tree, had sexual intercourse by putting me on top of his penis. I think at that moment I literally blacked out because I did not feel anything and only noticed the tree lights. I was then sent to bed. Poor, poor Destiny! She was only fourteen years old.

My father told me, that if I ever told anyone, that I would not live to see my sixteenth birthday. For the next year and a half, I lived in complete fear. My father continued to sexually molest me every chance he got with Carla right in the living room. Talking about being bold. It is amazing that predators, like him, prey on you when it is known that no one cared about you. This validated the fact that I was nothing; better yet, invisible. I only became visible when I was wanted for adult needs. Poor, poor Destiny!!

Being Fifteen

The Christmas, of her fifteenth birthday, was the first Christmas Destiny ever received gifts. It really bothered me that I had to watch my siblings have birthday parties and get stuff for Christmas. I was also a child and should been doing the same things. I received a ten-speed bike, and a recorder. My father continued to sexually molest me during this time.

On one occasion, during the summer of 1975, my father stated that my breasts were changing and that I should say something to Carla. I instead, decided to tell Carla about what was really going on. "He touches me every chance he gets." Her stepmother listened to what Destiny had to say. She, however, did not respond. Later that afternoon, when my father came home, my stepmother confronted him in front of me. Of course, he denied it. He even said she was the one who bought me the stuff for Christmas. Wow! I do not recall what happened after this, but, in September of 1975, I would faint at the corner store.

"Damaged Rhyme"

Mother Goose

Donald Duck

My stepmother got drunk

As I got fucked

She didn't fear

That I was ruined for life

She didn't care about my tears

She just wanted to be his wife

Just put her on punishment

Or kick her out the house

She is not worth the argument

She doesn't hold any clout

How can people act like they don't know

That a child never had a life

Instead of protecting her; treated her like a whoe

When her father did things, he did to his wife

At this point, no one loved me. I truly did not exist. I did not have the protection or love that a child needed to properly flourish. I never was told that I was nor loved. Even though there was an abundance of family to include aunts, uncles, cousins, etc., I was not important to protect.

I never had a pregnancy test, but all the adults decided I was pregnant. Prior to this, I used to like this guy Tony from school. He and I only had sex once. I told this to his mother, my mother and my stepmother. I was called a whore. My mother had told my father and Carla that I had asked her for some birth control pills. Everyone stated that I was a fast ass and should have not been thinking about sex. Interesting, I was being fucked by my father, sought after by other grown men, yet I should not be thinking of sex. My father did not say a word.

My mother, Carla, and I went around to my soon to be baby daddy's house. He was told that I was pregnant. Tony denied that he ever slept with me and his mother supported him. The conversation continued and before we left, everyone decided that I will have an abortion. I truly felt invisible and alone. This decision was made as if I wasn't there. I was not only scared, but I was totally invisible.

All I remember, after that, is going to school on a Friday, standing in the pretzel line with a school friend. I felt my baby moved. I knew that I would not be having an abortion. I ended up running away from home and all my problems. I would continue to learn that people use you according to what they want from you. I think I just wanted to know that someone saw me as a little brown girl. I think I wanted someone to care for me. I learned the truth; no one knew that I existed or even cared.

Changing Places

Prior to this situation, many people knew about the way that I was being treated at home. There were adult cousins, uncles, and friends who touched me whenever they got a chance. I would later find out that others knew but no one stepped in to protect me or to make me safe. I will never forget the hurtful things that were said to or about me. I was called all kinds of bitches and whores by grown ass women. Carla even threatened to put her foot up my ass. No one did not care that I was terrified!

"It Had to Happen to Me"

Why did it happen to me

Why was I punished so

I can't seem to get a grip on things

No matter how much I know

The holidays are arising

I feel so much anger and so much pain

Because the man who is my father

Had so much to gain

Does he realize he claimed he was drunk

When he screwed me

When he said he was drunk

But forgot when he was sober

When I was in the kitchen

And my stepmother on the sofa

How he would threaten and scare me

As he put his fingers in my pants

He said I wouldn't live to be sixteen

If I told anyone; not even my aunt

How he got so much pleasure

By causing me so much pain

He even told his buddies

Down at the bar, in the rain

Now every Christmas

And every New Year

I feel hurt, angry, sorrow, and grief

Because he took away my childhood years

I continued to attend school even though I was a runaway. Simon Gratz High, at the time, taught classes in the basement for the pregnant girls. I guess this was done to not corrupt the other children. I, however, chose to go to my regular classes even though some of my teachers didn't like it. I recall speaking to a school nurse or counselor about my situation. I was told about this home for unwed mothers. It was called Florence Crittenden Services. I would later learn about the role of this place.

After being a runaway for about five weeks, I decided to call my mother. She told me that the only way she would have anything to do with me is if I turn myself in to the police. I did. I was later taken to the Youth Study Center. I was in a cell that had a clear window. I shared this room with another pregnant girl. I was fifteen and very afraid. I would go to see a judge to figure out where I would go from this place. It was mentioned about the home for unwed mothers. I was approved to attend. I became a ward of the State and was sent to stay with an aunt while I waited for a bed at FCS.

The stay at my Aunt Jackie's house was just as crazy. My aunt, who had a baby boy, was one of my father's sisters. The funny thing is, prior to me staying with her, I don't ever recall seeing her. During this stay, I would have my sixteenth birthday at her house. I do not recall anything special except that my father brought me a coat to the house.

I do not remember too much about that time, but I thought everything was going fine. I knew that I would only be at my aunt's until I got placed but I was not prepared for the changes in her home.

One day, I overheard Aunt Jackie on the phone with another one of my aunts. I think up until this point, my aunt never knew why I was at her house. The aunt, on the phone, informed my aunt that I lied on my father and made up some story about him touching me. Her attitude changed and then she made a comment that she better go before I would accuse her husband of doing something to me. Again, Destiny would have to continue life as an invisible brown girl.

Journey of an invisible brown girl

Hidden

The time finally came for me to go to live at Florence Crittenden Services. This place was in the Germantown section of Philadelphia. It was like two houses connected. The buildings had offices, a kitchen, a daycare as well as a dining area. The rest were rooms that housed the pregnant girls. These girls were sent here while pregnant. They normally were gone after three months of giving birth. Once having their babies, they were either sent back home or to a foster home without their babies. Many had put their babies up for adoption. I would later learn, many years later, that Florence Crittenden Services was a place parents would send their pregnant daughters. Instead of providing care to their daughters, they would hide them, so they would not embarrass them. This was an inhumane method of dealing with unwed mothers.

Somewhere between the 1950s and 1970s, places like Florence Crittenden Services, were to pressure, coerced, and scare young unwed mothers into giving up their babies to married couples. These families were unable to conceive their own baby. So, now being taught that they were an embarrassment to their families and friends, these unwed mothers were taught giving their babies away would make things right again. Many, of these young unwed mothers, exchanged their babies for gifts and money. I was already invisible, so this was the perfect place. The counselors also tried to get Destiny to put her child up for adoption because after all, she was not wanted, nor did she have any place to go. Destiny really did not know what to do. She was so hurt, scared, and alone.

I recall seeing two older girls at FCS with their babies. They seemed to be very experienced with the babies. This was the first time I saw someone breastfeeding. I found it to be amazing that milk would come out of the breast. I wanted to try this once having my baby. I really did not know where my life was going, but, I did realize that I had no one. It was like I just vanished into air. I was invisible. My family did not have anything to do with me. I really did not know what to expect, but life was happening. I want to say this: All of the motherfuckers who belittled, isolated, abuse, ignored, and mistreated me, will truly pay the price. The name calling was just as horrible as being hit. I was called bitches, whores, and sluts by grown ass women. There were all kinds of things said about me. Of the people I knew, I was the only one pregnant. My only two childhood friends disappeared. I was here on this earth alone with no one to care, love or protect me.

I was in the home with other girls who were also pregnant and invisible. We became the family or friends and support system for each other. We had chores to do, as well as, continue to attend school. There also was a curfew we had to follow. We also had fun. I continued to attend my regular school up until I had my baby. My pregnancy was going fine except for morning sickness. This usually happened whenever I ate eggs. It was amazing to feel the movement of my baby inside of me. I also had the chore of cooking and helping with the meals for the house. I loved it. The kitchen was huge and helped develop me into a great cook. I also was great at sewing. I do not know where I learned these skills. Maybe I learned these things in home economics' class. The first thing I had learned to cook was a tuna casserole. The first thing I learned how to sew was a pillow.

The girls, at FCS, earned an allowance while there. Some of us would do down to this steak place, called the Dugout, on Fridays. They had the best cheesesteaks. There were other girls, who did not live at FCS, who also would come to the house. I became friends with one. Sharon and I would become lifetime best friends. I wonder whatever happened to the girls once they left? What are they doing with themselves today?

A Child is Born

You are the first, a baby girl

A beautiful jewel of the night

I was only sixteen, left alone in this world

Learning to fight, to keep you in my life

Destiny went into labor in March. I was terrified and in so much pain. I was also alone. I gave birth to a bouncing baby girl. She weighed in at 5 pounds and 7 ounces. My daughter was the most beautiful baby I had ever seen. I also had the opportunity to breastfeed her. During my stay at the hospital, I still did not know what was going to happen now that I had my baby. I later would find out that my mother had sign the papers for me to put my daughter away. She was willing to bring me home but not with a baby. I do not know where or how, but, I ended up calling a counselor at FCS and begged to stay with my baby. They said okay. I was the first one able to live there with a baby. I stayed until I finished high school, with my baby, and my leaving was my choice. I just might have a chance in life.

There was a lot for Destiny to learn as a new mother. She breastfed her daughter for a few weeks until she returned to school. I had my own room with my baby. I received a $9 weekly allowance. This was for me to buy whatever my baby would need. I learned how to make baby food, how to use and wash cloth diapers as well as make carnation baby formula. Again, even though she had her own baby, Destiny was still hurting from the abandonment of her family and friends. No one kept in contact with her. It was like she just disappeared. After all, Destiny was only sixteen years old.

New Chance

I stayed at FCS for two tears. During this time,
Destiny continued to go to school and even went on her
prom. I didn't know the boy. He was a relative of one
of the counselors. I made my own gown and had fun.
Everyone, at FCS, did their best to make sure I had a
great time. There were many things that I would
experience but I longed for the love of family and
friends or someone to love me. I also still longed for
my baby daddy even though he denied my daughter. I
had a hard time understanding why he was acting funny
towards me. I was so anxious for him to see his
daughter. I would go to his street, so my friends could
see the baby. Once they would see her, they would tell

him, but I was just a joke. I had hoped to run into him but with no luck. He would deny her for two years.

I do remember, that prior to finishing school, I started seeing Billy. He would later become my baby daddy number two. I had enjoyed spending time with him especially because he came from a large family. This was something I had wanted. Everyone seemed to like my daughter and me. I would later move in with them. I still did not have connection with my family nor do I remember at what point my mother would see my daughter. Not only did I have a place to stay, but, I was also free to do whatever I wanted to do. Welfare, W.I.C., partying, etc.; what more could I ask for? By the time she was eighteen, Destiny had been pregnant twice.

I do not know when I got pregnant or how far I was, but my second pregnancy would end in a miscarriage. I was devastated. I cried and cried and cried. After all, I was not quite eighteen. I had gone to the grocery store earlier that day and had pulled the shopping cart up two flights of stairs. Later, I would start spotting and my water broke. I went to the hospital to see what was going on. The hospital had me convinced that I was about to have a baby. I went to the bathroom and a big lump of something fell out. I told the nurse and she said that was normal. It wasn't; it was my baby.

Anyway, after the miscarriage, I came home and became depressed. Each time I had a period or saw a baby, I would get depressed. I eventually would get pregnant again, however, my relationship with baby daddy number two was changing.

I would constantly be picked on. Billy would accuse me of looking at other men including his brothers. It seemed like I was always afraid of something. Baby daddy number two and I would eventually move into our own place together.

I remember, somewhere during this pregnancy, my mother started threatening me about taking my first daughter. She would tell me stuff like, "A child is supposed to have three outfits a day and you are not a good mother." It is amazing, because, this was the same woman who signed the papers to have my daughter put away. I still feared my mother. She ended up getting my daughter. It was not to help me, but, to hurt me. After all, I was still afraid of my mother and did not know what to do. My daughter was about two years old. I do not know how long she had her, but my heart was hurting.

Next came you, a little pearl

It is true that I ws18 years young

Even without the support from the world

I have more than enough love to make life for you fun

In July 1978, Destiny gave birth to her second daughter. She came into the world early weighing 4 pounds and 11 ounces. I was so happy. My pregnancy was considered high risk because my body was containing too much amniotic fluid. This was causing me to go into early labor. I did not think I was going to have a baby because of this issue. I was having flashbacks of my last pregnancy. I was eighteen years old and had already been pregnant for the third time. I would have to go to the doctor's office every few weeks to have the fluid drained. It was an uncomfortable procedure that felt like a balloon was to burst every time they inserted the needle. I would also breastfeed my baby for a few weeks.

My relationship, with baby daddy number two, did not get any better. We would break up around my daughter's second birthday. It is amazing, as people judged you for the things you do, they forget the things they have done or doing in their own life. I had to make many decisions, about life, that I really did not know anything about. I did not have any help and found myself with no place to go. I remember, after asking for help, I ended up staying at the Salvation Army overnight. I was told that I would not be able to

stay longer. I do not remember the reason they gave me, but come the next day, I would be homeless. Talk about something scary. Destiny had a baby and nowhere to go. I did not have any assistance from her father. I would later find refuge with someone that I thought was my friend. That, however, was also a lie.

Crooked Help

I stayed with a sister of some school friends of mine. Dena had three children of her own. She would leave, for weeks, without her children. Dena only came home when it was time for her to get her food stamps and welfare check. I would be stuck taking care of her children with no funds from her. This went on for a while. I could not do anything because I did not have any place to go. I would finally get a place of my own. It was a run down, roach infested place; but it was mine. The thing I promised myself, when I moved in, was that I would never allow myself to get into a situation where I would worry about a place to live.

I continued to date during this time. I still had the longing for Tony but continued with my life. I was trying to enjoy my life. My first daughter was back in my life with my other daughter. Somewhere along the lines, her father decided to accept her as his child. She would go back and forth between our home and her father's mother's house. In the meantime, he continually belittled me and talked down about me to everyone. He also made it seem like he was so much better than everyone and that I was some low life person because I chose to keep my daughter. He lived in luxury places and drove luxury cars while his daughter would be at his mother's house. I still had wished that he would pay me some mind.

I began seeing James. I enjoyed being with him and he would eventually move in with me. During this time, I became pregnant with my third child. Yes, I was on my third baby daddy and was living my life. I finally thought that I had someone who cared for me. However, I didn't know what that meant.

Baby daddy number three would always be in the streets hanging out with his boys. I recalled, one day, that my first daughter had set a sock on fire in our apartment. Instead of discipling her with a belt, I hit her in her face causing a black eye. My daughter had gone around her grandmother's house to show them her eye. Tony came to my house. I was home alone. He basically threatened me as well as slapped me in the face. He stated that he did not care that I was pregnant and that I better let him in whenever he would come around. That really was a punk move. He knew I was home alone, he knew that no one would have my back as well as that I was timid. He would come pass the next day. I, however, was ready. I was doing my daughter's hair with a machete next to me in the event he would try to hit me. My daughter was six years old and observed everything that was taking place. She would years later say that he whipped my ass. No, he didn't. Everything would end peacefully.

Daughter number one would go back and forth between my place and her grandmother's house. She did what most children did by playing her parents against each other to do what she wanted to do. Financially, I was not getting any help for my children. I had no contact with baby daddy number two. Baby daddy number one would play another real punk move. He was struggling financially and decided that he needed his daughter to get a welfare check. This check would allow him to continue to live his lavish life. Again, this was not done to help me, but to hurt me. People knew when no one cares for you because they take advantage of you and treat you any kind of way. As of today, I cannot stand people who treat other people this kind of way.

A bouncing baby boy is number three

At age 23, becoming better at standing on my own

I thank God for you, the gift He gave to me

The pleasure I have watching you

As I learn to become grown

Destiny went into labor in July of 1982. I was in labor for twenty-four hours. Baby daddy number three was present when our son was born. I would breastfeed my son till he was about a year old. Life appeared to be fine. I now had three children. Still no help, love or support from my family. Did people really think I vanished?

There were plenty of children on my block. They were always at my house helping with my children and doing things around the house. I would take these children places I would go. Baby daddy number three was still living with me but things were about to change.

On one night, after drinking with his boys, James came home upset. He asked me why I didn't tell him about my father? His friends informed him that my father had sex with me. He told me that my father would go to the local bar and tell the things he was doing to me. Wow! This was my confirmation that other people did know yet did not care to protect me or make me safe. No one took the time to know me because I truly did not matter. Just as I thought that I was learning to go on with my life, despite my past, I was stuck.

Eventually, baby daddy number three and I would break up. I had three children, by three different men, no help and did not have the time to raise a man. He had to go!

Truly Denied

Being called all types of things

Getting put down by everyone

Teaching you to be queens and king

Raising you, my children, with little help or none

Destiny was very promiscuous (as society would call her) as well as had a few abortions. Always thinking that someone would want me for me. Hoping that someone would want me for me. Even the few female friends I had, always made it seem like they were better than me. They would make comments that other people wanted to know why they would hang out with someone like me. Why, because I had children or couldn't get the materialistic things that they had? I could not afford to by name brand or expensive things. I did not live with my family and I had children to care for. This included food, bills, etc., etc. Were they really doing me a favor? I felt so at that time. I was still young and felt I was damaged goods not worthy of anything good. I was to make them feel better about themselves when I was around. This is not something that friends should do or say. It would take me many years before I learned this lesson!

My mother would also continue to bully me and say hurtful things such as, "no man wants a woman with kids by different men or you will never be nothing." I never felt like I was pretty because others would act like they were better than me. They weren't! Just because a woman doesn't have children, does not mean she isn't fucking or never got pregnant! Some also were getting their ass beat by their men. I did not know it then, but, I was constantly bullied or taken advantage by someone because I thought I did not deserve better. Not one person stepped in to help or school me. I had dealt with men who enjoyed sleeping with me but did not think I was worthy for a good life.

I had no clue who I was, but I was determined to search for me. First, real men do accept other men's children if he is in love with their mother. Life is not based on a woman having a man in her life. Having a man who beats your ass, doesn't contribute financially or help with the children would have not worked for me!

I was not receiving any help from none of my baby daddies. My first daughter was still going back and forth between me and her grandmother's house. My other two baby daddies did not have any involvement with their children. I had to make a change.

I had always thought that there was more to life than this mess that I was experiencing. Destiny decided to go back to school. Even though I was still in my twenties, I had an 8, 6 as well as a 2-year-old to raise and wanted more than just welfare. This was a good move for me. Welfare provided me with help such as childcare, transportation as well as school supplies. My daughters were in elementary school while my son was in daycare. During this time, I would run into baby daddy number two's brother. I informed him that I really needed help with my daughter. By the end of 1985 or before 1986, baby daddy number two came around. He was not happy. He told me, "The only person you cared about is your son and improving yourself." Who wouldn't want to improve themselves? He also said, "Your son will be the one to grow up and break your heart." First, let's get this straight: every child has two parents. They are both suppose to provide financially as well as emotionally to their child; not just when they are involved with each other.

Also, the one who would grow up to break my heart would be daughter number one. (We will talk about this a little later). He left with his daughter. I never knew where she was nor did not have a way of contacting her. Daughter number two would be a teenager the next time that I would hear from her.

Things were going great with school. My grades were good, and I began to come out of my shell. I was the president of student council and had made some friends. I was now ready to finish up with an Associate in Business Administration/Accounting. The night before my graduation, my friends and I went out to celebrate. On our way home, we were in a terrible car accident. One of my so- called friends pulled me on her for protection. I was really injured. I had glass under my eye and in my arm. I, however, was determined to make it to my graduation. I worked hard for this and graduating with honors was something I did not want to miss. My mother stated that she did not know I was that smart. I had received some scholarships for schools but instead chose to work. I was determined to leave the hood and come off welfare.

I received a settlement from the accident. This allowed me to leave the hood. Finally! Prior to me leaving, one of the neighborhood's children's mother became addicted to drugs. This left her children trying to find means to survive. I helped when I could by bringing them with me. I always had it in my heart to share my good with others. I do not know where this came from because no one didn't share with me and I was still invisible to people.

Changing Things

The next few years continued to be challenging. I was working at the post office. I also was driving and had my own car. Destiny was finally off welfare and out of the hood. I would continue to form a relationship with my sister. Carla would have another daughter by my father. I would hang out with my first sister and her friend. We thought we were the rapping group Salt n Peppa. We really had fun with each other.

During this time, I had my first daughter and son with me. They had attended the school in our neighborhood. I was still trying to prove to my mother that I was good enough to be her daughter. However, she still did not really care for me or my children. Another lie was transforming during this time.

I was still hanging out with the friends of mine from my old neighborhood. As time went on, my female friend would start making comments like, "Just because someone offers to pay for you, doesn't mean you have to accept it." Wow! So, things were getting tense. Erica and Jason would have a son but would eventually break up. I do not know the reason why, but it was always a violent relationship. Jason was always beating Erica for something. I heard about it but witness his abuse once. We were walking to Erica's house when they got into something. I called myself stepping in to defend Erica. Jason stepped to me, but he never put his hands on me. I was scared but I stood up to him.

I was supposed to be the baby's godmother, but I never got to meet my godson. Now, this is when things became tricky. After they broke up, Jason would begin to pursue me. We dated for a minute or just began to have sex. He never disrespected me and offered me support when I needed it. Hell, no one had ever done this for me. I never thought of the implications of the relationship with Erica. I also did not know that there was a rule in place when people you know break up. I would later find out that Erica would belittle me to others every chance she got. I ended up losing contact with both. It was better for me.

Not Again

Moving out of the hood was a good move for me. The teenager, that I was caring for, would later return to her family. My oldest daughter would graduate from middle school. There still was no word from my second daughter. I was still working at the post office and would later get a job in New Jersey working at the new Taj Mahal Casino. I was also still dating. I started seeing this young guy, Stan, who was in the military. We really did not get along. Do believe this saying: "When someone shows you their true colors, believe them." He would always talk about his model friends that were thinner than me. Another person that acted like they were better than me and doing me a favor. I was changing but still moving slow to this type of mess. I was offended but continue to see him. We would eventually move in together. Because of my job, we would later move to New Jersey.

Once moving to New Jersey, our relationship did not improve, and we decided to break up. As usual, I had no problem dating. I really did not have any value of myself because I always dated guys that wanted other women. Even though I had always used birth control pills, I would end up pregnant. It was a surprise this time because my last child was eight years old. My life was different now. I was living in a nice place and enjoyed my job.

I informed Stan that I was pregnant. He previously told me that he could not have any children because of a health issue. Even though he knew that I had dated someone else, he offered to marry me. I accepted. I now was about to have my fourth baby, at thirty-one years old, by another baby daddy, but this time, he would be my husband. My mother would be wrong again. A man did want to marry me with children by another man. Again, I was still being judged. Just because a woman doesn't have any children, does not mean she was not fucking! She could have had an abortion or just was not able to get pregnant. Some women even put their babies up for adoption or had other people raise their children. They were not better than me. I just chose to have my children.

Beautiful number four

With your head full of hair

31 when I had you, raising you has made life so much fun

Cuddly and soft like a teddy bear

I am so glad you are in my life, with you I feel I have won

My son was born in January of 1991. I was alone when I went into labor. My husband had been sent to Iraq for war. No one really did not notice me. I thought things would be different because I was married. I still lived an invisible brown girl survival life, with children, but now married. I had put everything into my children. I had matured and became better at being a mom. My first daughter and I were having a lot of problems. I could not find anyone to help me. She was now sixteen and was really acting out. It was amazing to me that the people who took her away from me when she was younger, would not help. I found a tough love program for her. She stayed there for about 28 days. I would later get help from the woman, whose children I helped, while she was strung out on drugs.

Once Stan came home, we were relocated to North Carolina. This place was culture shock to me. There were no stores, no transportation and we only had my car. I had to be like the oldest military bride. Most of these brides were barely in their twenties. I was in my thirties. My husband would take the car for work. I had two children with me, no car and I felt trapped.

My husband and I still did not get along. I went to go get my tubes tied and I was told that not only did I need my husband's signature, but there was also a waiting list. What? This was some crazy mess. It is interesting, that even though many men don't want to be responsible for their children, if they can trap you; they will.

Destiny had just finished weaning her fourth child, when she started feeling terrible. I thought it was the stress of everything. I went to the doctor thinking maybe I would need some iron or something, but to my surprise, I was told something else. Yup, I was pregnant again. I really felt like fertile myrtle. The judgmental attitudes started back up. People, who didn't care if I existed, would comment on me being pregnant. I made sure that I would be getting my tubes tied after this baby. Now, I want to say this; many brown girls keep their babies compared to other groups. The thought never crossed my mind to abort all my babies nor did it make sense for me to put them up for adoption. I also noticed that my maturity level was completely different from when I was a teen mother. I knew how I wanted to have my baby as well as how I would care for my baby. It seemed like the only way invisible brown girls are visible, is when others want to put them down.

Destiny's last son was premature and born December of 1992. I was only in labor for about fifteen minutes. By the time I reached the hospital, had my water broke, he was here. I had delivered him in the bed before the medical staff returned.

At age 33, you were given to me

My little knight always seeking more

A duplicate of my intelligence, competiness, and creativity

Always by my side when others walk out

I have made the right choice for sure

A few days after having her baby, Destiny would learn she made a mistake in getting married. Stan felt that taking care of his household was too much even though Destiny just gave birth a few days ago. There was no time for me to heal and recuperate. I want to say, that the world appears to be different when you come from a background where people deal with you like you never existed. You live your life in total isolation, especially if you are not a follower. Somewhere along the line, I stopped believing in people and became on my own path. This didn't mean I didn't want a decent life and to be loved. I never asked anyone for help raising my children or me, but it didn't stop the name calling and mistreatment.

I was away from the only place I knew, at home with three children, no car, and no help. My husband would take the only car for work or church. Let me say this, it is amazing when young women or girls, have babies, they are made to feel worthless. Whether you are married or not, no one looks at the baby daddy. Of course, this would be another relationship I would end. I had given birth to five children, three with me, and still carrying the burden of being condoned as a young, unwed mother. After eight years of marriage, I found myself still a single mother raising children alone.

Intermission

Growing from an unwanted invisible child to an adult can be a challenge but it can be done. So much time is spent along the way trying to prove that you are good enough. It is even more challenging if you are a young mother. Somehow, society has it that you are fast and loose. I have heard many women claim they only slept with one man, or their body is too delicate to have many babies or something that makes them think they are better than you. What does that have to do with the color of paint? Don't believe it. Everyone has a different story. Only God knows the truth. This does not give any woman the right to treat a young and unwed mother like crap. Your untruth of yourself is affecting the being of others. Trust me, you are not doing us a favor.

An invisible brown girl is only visible when people want something from you. I found that brown women are the worse when dealing with invisible brown girls. They hide behind these brown girls. So, instead of encouraging them, building them up, they remind them of their past. They make it seem like many of these invisible brown girls deserve it.

Many brown women are trying so hard to hold on to their image, their status, and their men despite of how he treats them. I began to lose the taste for men and the women that love them. It took me years to learn that many brown women were lying about themselves. Some were being physically abused by their men. Others had men that cheated on them on a regular basis. Some had to depend on these same men to financially provide for them leaving them to accept their behavior. Hiding behind their churches and communities instead of getting help for themselves. Why take out your hurt, pain, and anger on a young brown girl?

The experiences, of dealing with insecure and thoughtless individuals, make life even more difficult for invisible brown girls. You can never do anything right. Much time is spent looking for someone to help ease the pain of being unwanted. You start out tip toeing around about yourself only to have someone slam you in your face. Do believe, you can stop all this madness. However, for Destiny, she would have to experience more things.

Waking Up

Ending her marriage left Destiny with very low self-esteem. I felt ashamed for having five children and no baby daddy. Even though the choices I made, to end the relationship with my baby daddies were valid to me, society didn't see it my way. As often, the mothers are left feeling cheap, like crap while the baby daddies are given an "okay to pursue your life" card. They do not have to justify why they stop caring for their children. It is even funny that other women support them without pushing them to be fathers to their children. The mother must figure out where she will get the means to provide for the children. I also want to make something else clear: every baby momma does not sleep with her baby daddy! Once a relationship is over, the only thing that parents have in common and must do are the things that pertain to the children. The name calling and mistreatment that I had endured was now being force on my children. Name calling, nasty remarks and disgracing their mother had become a way of life. And others believed it. I remember a coworker telling me that my Stan told him the things that were going on and he wasn't doing what he was supposed to do. Because he was in the church, he was forgiven. I tried, to the best of my ability, to let my children know that they are loved and can be whatever they want. I, also, never belittled their fathers to them. I allowed them to make their own decisions when it came to their fathers.

I became involved with a family that really made me feel worse about myself. They made me feel stupid whenever I cried about things that hurt my feelings. They constantly reminded me of my past and kept me down. I was involved with the youngest son for six years when he got another woman pregnant. I was devastated. He was not right for me, but my self-esteem was telling me otherwise. He would occasionally buy me food to eat and buy things for me. It was the cheap things. I also didn't learn this to later. The tricks that your mind play on you when you have low self-esteem. Even though I was a very intelligent person, I was reminded that I was less than dirt and street naive.

He took me to a place, about eight hours away, to tell me that he got someone pregnant. During this time, he would belittle me and say all types of nasty things to me to downplay the mess he had done. My heart was broken into pieces.

To You

You said you loved me

You said you cared

But when I needed you

You weren't there

You couldn't be content with just me

I wasn't enough flame or was I just a fad

I changed that, I was more than enough

There were just others you had to have

You said I was a crybaby

When my feelings were hurt

What difference did it make to you

To you I was less than dirt

What have I done to you

For you to treat me this way

All I ever wanted was for you to be true

You didn't care, you just wanted to play

You leave me in tears

Why do you hate me so

Am I paying for the years

Others had you blow

I can't sleep and eat

All I do is cry

But I'll get over this

As for now, my heart just died

He really made me feel like I was nothing but an old barren woman who failed at giving him a child. Not only was I better than good enough, but I already gave birth to five children. No way was I barren but when you have no self-esteem, anything makes sense. I lost over twenty pounds in a month from crying. I really thought that I was less than life. I thought that I had failed at giving him a child. If only I hadn't got my tubes tied. I beat myself up something terrible. I allowed his mother to put me down by saying things like she wanted a grandchild and that I already had children or that other women would deal with it. Wow! These women evidently had low self-esteem as well. They also got the neighborhood involved to the point anytime there was an event, the baby's mother was invited. These older women were just hags. My heart continuously broke over and over. I would later end the relationship.

Now, I know many of you will say that this couldn't be you. Unless you have walked in my shoes, you don't know. I have always been intelligent, but life had dealt me some stuff making me feel real dumb. Not knowing when people were throwing breeze or just being bullies wasn't that simple to me. I always thought the best of people yet couldn't understand why they would treat me wrong. Trying to hold on had been hard. I never learned how to get loud with people. Matter of fact, I was seen more as a crybaby than anything else. I really did not know what else to do beside fucking somebody up. I was too scared to make a move. Not because I thought I would get beat up, but, because no one would like me. I would be in my fifties before I changed the game. Invisibility would have a new meaning to me.

Blooming

Destiny still dated but her views on men had changed. I dealt with them for sex and money, but I did not get into a relationship. I started becoming arrogant and very outspoken. I began to change from the girl who was withdrawn and invisible. I changed to become a woman whom was secure, beautiful, and living life. I no longer cared whether others wanted to be bother with me. I am the way that very few people will ever be. My focus was spending time with my children and grandchildren.

I became more verbal about things that would affect me. I had gone back to school to obtain my bachelor and master's degrees. I started traveling and really enjoying my life. I even got married two more times. I, however, would not tolerate anyone hurting me. I also decided to put closure to some things that had affected my growth. I have reached a point in my life that everyone will have to answer to something much greater than me.

I decided to have a relationship with my mother. It was hard for me, at first, because she still was trying to bully me. I, at first, still feared her even though I was a grown woman. I continued to visit my mother whenever I was in the area. We also started communicating more on the telephone. Somewhere along the line, I reminded myself that I will not fear anyone. This change many things for me. My mother and I have traveled together and enjoy talking to each other. She has recently told me that she has regret not hugging and kissing my brother and me. She wished she could have done things differently with us. My mother did say that there are no perfect parents. This is true but, my life, as a child was horrible. However, I learned that her hate, anger, and bitterness came from her past and how she was treated by her mother. It is sad that she never learned to forgive and move on. I am so sorry she had to experience this type of treatment, but it still does not justify her behavior towards the only two children she had. It is crucial that parents understand the things that go into the molding of their children. Generational curses cannot be broken until we come to terms about the things that have hurt us. Love, apologies, and forgiveness play a key role in raising children. The support, help, and love from others can go a long way. When one comes your way for help or guidance, this is not your time to brag, manipulate, or further abuse them. If things are going good for you, share your key of knowledge.

Men do understand, if you are actively involved with a woman who has children, you still have a role to play. If you see her with her children and you are laying between her legs, do something. No, they do not need another daddy and it is understood they are not your children, However, you can be a man by bringing over groceries, taking the boys to get haircuts or to sport events. These children will grow up and remember you to be the low life that only wanted to fuck their mother. Women, you also demand that from these men.

Another thing I learned is that people want you to think they have it going on when the truth of the matter is, they don't. All the judging, name calling, and belittling is to cover-up the things that were going on in their lives. See, when you are feeling bad, hurt or needing help, that instead of these people helping you, they end up beating you down. There is no such thing as perfect people. Do understand that those who really mean you well and are doing well, will not beat you down. Realize that once you stop being invisible, people will look different to you.

One day you look, and the caterpillar has turned into a beautiful butterfly. It has wings that will now make the journey easier. Its' wings display the many journeys it has made. They also carry forgiveness and love which it sprinkles wherever it goes. Wherever the butterfly goes, it is now celebrated. People even make gardens to attract it.

Like the butterfly, I sprinkle myself wherever I go. Only God has the credit for my life. I have no role models and do not credit no one for making me visible. I realize that I live everyday in color. This does not mean that I do not have challenges because I do. Now that I realize that no one has my best interest at heart, it does make it a challenge to deal with folks. I have spent so much time trying to get people to like me or to see me, that I was shutting me out. Stroking other people's egos, settling for the scraps others throw my way or even being mistreated by my children, made me wonder what was this all for? Even though I struggled through life, I always love my children.

I do not regret having any of you over no person

Having all of you has been the best decision I made

in my life

I feel pity for everyone

Making me feel stupid, used, dumb, and confused

They lost out and do not deserve none

Of the joy and the love, I have for my five jewels

However, my heart would break one more time!

Deception

Despite the many challenges in my life, the only thing I cared about are my children. I looked forward to our time together. I am excited about being a gmom to my grandchildren and ggmom to my great grandchildren. I couldn't understand what was going on. I didn't get pictures, cards, etc. like other families. Even though I felt this wasn't right, I continued to see everyone. No matter where I lived, I always came to see my mother and children. I felt deep down that I wasn't treated right but chose to ignore these feelings. After all, everything I sacrificed in my life was for my children. I continued to come around for at least twenty years. By this time, my children were grown. I spent money on traveling to them, money on food or whatever was going on as well as bringing goodies. Feeling like I was buying for them to like me and thinking they loved me until one day, my oldest daughter dropped the bomb on me. I was not feeling well, and she called to see how I was doing. It turned out, she had other plans. My child belittled me over something that took place when she was six years old.

She told me things that others told her about me. After cursing and screaming at me, my child hung the phone up on me. Wow! Everything that Destiny fought for, with her children, was all for nothing. She couldn't believe it, but, everything now made sense. I understood why I wasn't treated like mother of the year or never received any help the few times I asked. Again, I was totally ignored like I never existed. I was still invisible, even to my children. Treated like I never loved them or cared for them. The lies that were told, from others about me, meant more to my child than the truth. I wrote my daughter a nine-page letter, but it didn't matter. I also realized, at that moment, that I would stop justifying everything about me. I realized that no one really loved or cared for me. The only thing that matter, was the things I could give or do for them.

After picking up my heart, I decided it was okay for me to heal. I wrote a list of past lovers, known enemies and notes to those who have caused me harm, whether knowingly or not. I then prayed for them and then burned the paper to release. I decided to give it to God and release my hurt. This is about my healing; my journey. I am okay with not being the perfect daughter, the perfect woman, wife, grandmother, great grandmother or mother. It is okay that I am intelligent, imperfect, creative, emotional, free-spirited, wild and beautiful. It is okay to not be liked, not like others as well as being invisible if chosen. This is my journey. There is much more to come in this journey. A new journey begins.

Looking Out My Window

As I sit, looking out my window

I think of the times

That are now like a shadow

I think of the trends

How different, how unreal, how complicated

Things must have been

For a child to learn at an early age

How bad things will be

Only to grow to a mature stage

To learn how things will stay

How we live day to day

Behind happy faces

While losing our health and our minds

Trying to put our true feelings in their [laces

These things I think of

As I look out the window

As I continue this journey, I advise all of those who mistreated me, to dig down deep into your own souls and come to term with your own mess. Get the fuck out of mines. Making one invisible because of your own demons is no longer acceptable to me. No one never knew me or the beautiful soul I am and never will. That is your loss. From here and to the end, I will be a wild and free-spirited woman. My new journey starts today. My life is defined by me. My past no longer has me. This journey is truly amazing!

Signed

Destiny, Retired Invisible Brown Girl

*Update- I would later find out that it was daughter number two that created the deception. What was so amazing is during the time that I was hurting over the things my first daughter said, daughter number two tried to inform me. How much she was happy about our relationship. She never told me that she was the one to get my daughter started with the lies of me not wanting them and abusing them. When people are miserable with themselves, they look for others to join them. Don't allow yourself to get trapped by their mess. Snakes will bite anyone! *

Author Cherrel Turner-Callwood actively enjoys writing. She has previously published her first children's book "The Adventures of Chocolate Sunshine". She looks forward to publishing more books soon. The author is currently enjoying retired life on the beaches of Florida.